The Perfect Prince

by Paul Harrison

illustrated by Sue Mason

READZONE

There was once a princess named Isabella. Like all princesses, she was expected to meet a handsome prince, fall in love and have a baby or two.

Unfortunately, Isabella didn't meet any princes she liked.

"How about this one?" her mother, the queen, would ask.

"No, not that one," she would reply.

She always said no. They were
either too tall, or too small, or too fat,
or too thin, or too clever, or too
stupid, or too foolish, or too boring.
They were never the perfect prince.

So Isabella went for long
walks to avoid all the
unsuitable suitors.

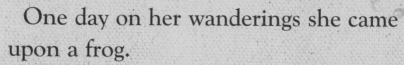

One day on her wanderings she came upon a frog.

Now, from the stories, she knew that when princesses kiss frogs there is a bit of magic and, hey-presto, the perfect prince appears in front of them.

So Isabella thought she'd give it a go.
She kissed the frog. Nothing happened.
The frog didn't turn into a prince.
Instead it stayed just as froggy as before.

By the time she got back home to the palace, Isabella was looking a little green.

"Are you well, dear?" asked her father, the king.

"Croak," she replied.

"She must have a cold," said her mother.

17

That night at
supper, Princess
Isabella didn't eat
a thing.

19

Until she saw the fly. Out shot her tongue, and in went the fly.

"Oooh, disgusting!" said her mother.

"Yum!" thought Isabella.

21

Isabella was sent straight to bed, so off she hopped up the stairs.

22

23

That night strange things
happened in the palace.
Magical things.

In the morning, her parents came to wake her. But Isabella was nowhere to be seen.

Instead, in the middle of her bed, sat a frog.

"Yuck!" screamed the queen. "Get rid of that

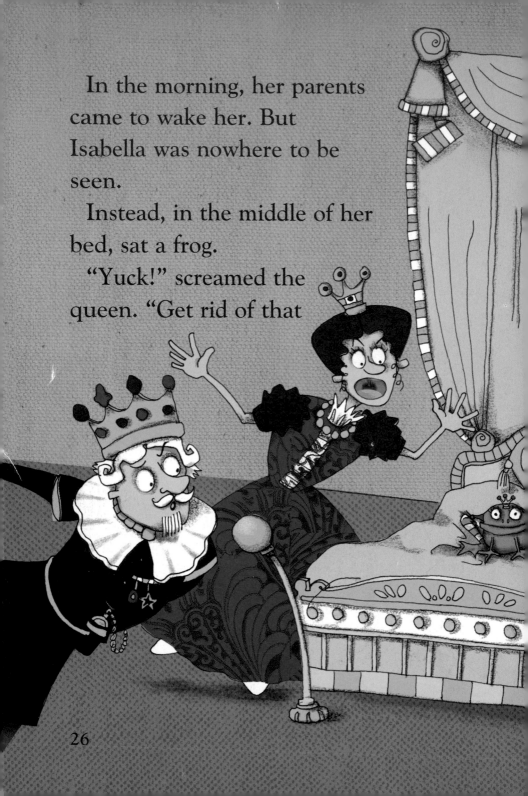

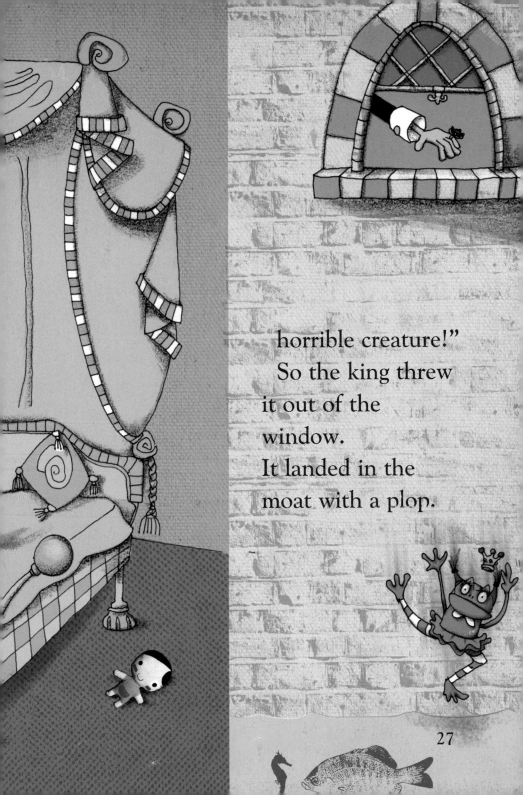

horrible creature!"
So the king threw
it out of the
window.
It landed in the
moat with a plop.

But that frog was no ordinary frog.
Of course, it was really Isabella.

Not that she could tell anyone who she really was. She could only croak.

Was she sad? Not at all. Being a frog meant no more soppy princes.

They fell in love and
had some babies.
About three thousand of them!

Did you enjoy this book?

Look out for more *Swifts* titles –
stories in 500 words